June 2013

To: Ty
From: Grammy

The Boxcar Children® Mysteries

THE GROWLING BEAR MYSTERY

created by
GERTRUDE CHANDLER WARNER

Illustrated by Charles Tang

ALBERT WHITMAN & Company
Morton Grove, Illinois

Library of Congress Cataloging-in-Publication Data

Warner, Gertrude Chandler, 1890–
The growling bear mystery/created by Gertrude Chandler Warner;
illustrated by Charles Tang.
p. cm —(The Boxcar children mysteries)
Summary: When the Aldens visit Yellowstone they discover a map showing
the way to the old cabin where gold is supposedly hidden, but they
encounter lots of interference in their attempts to hike the trail.
ISBN 0-8075-3070-0 (hardcover)
ISBN 0-8075-3071-9 (paperback)
[1. Yellowstone National Park–Fiction. 2. Brother sand sisters–Fiction.
3. Hiking–Fiction. 4. Orphans–Fiction. 5. Mystery and detective stories.]
I. Tang, Charles, ill. II. Title.
III. Series: Warner, Gertrude Chandler, 1890–
Boxcar children mysteries.
PZ7.W244Gr 1997   97-40302
[Fic]–dc21   CIP
                                           AC

Cover art by David Cunningham.

Contents

CHAPTER 1

On Top of the World

The four Alden children posed for a picture in front of a log sign. The sign was tall, even taller than Henry, the oldest of the children.

The youngest Alden, six-year-old Benny, sandwiched himself between his two older sisters, Jessie and Violet. He smiled for his grandfather's camera. "Cheese and crackers," Benny said, breaking into a grin.

"Hold those smiles," Mr. Alden called out. "I just ran out of film. Stay for a minute while I reload."

Jessie said to Henry, Violet, and Benny, "Let's move aside so these other tourists can take pictures in front of the sign, too."

Benny asked Jessie, "Why does everybody stop here to get pictures taken?"

Jessie was always full of information. "Well, Benny," she began, "we're standing on the Continental Divide. It runs along the top of the Rocky Mountains. On one side of the Divide, streams and rivers flow west to the Pacific Ocean. On the other side, they go east toward the Atlantic Ocean. The Continental Divide is famous. That's why people have their pictures taken here."

Benny squinted at the log sign. "I get it. If I pour my water bottle out right here, half the water will go one way, and the other half will go the other way."

"Why don't you try it and find out," Henry suggested.

Benny poured his water bottle onto the dry ground. "Hey, all my water disappeared into the ground!" he complained. "Which ocean would I go to if I rolled down this mountain?"

"I wouldn't try that, Benny," Violet said. "This mountain is pretty steep. My ears have been popping ever since we got off the plane."

Mr. Alden noticed that Benny was getting restless. He knew his grandson always wanted to get wherever they were going. "Hang on, Benny. We'll be in Yellowstone National Park shortly. Mrs. McGregor said she wants us to bring back plenty of snapshots from our trip. Let's stretch our legs a bit until it's our turn for pictures again."

The Aldens strolled to the edge of the lookout where they were parked. In front of them, the Rocky Mountains stretched in every direction.

Violet took a deep breath of air. "I love the smell of all these trees. I never saw such tall, skinny ones before."

Benny wanted to be walking through the trees, not sniffing them. "I wish we could try out our new hiking boots right now on this big mountain."

Henry gave Benny a friendly punch in the arm. "No chance of that. There's a chain across the trail. See the sign?"

"Lost Cabin Trails Closed," Benny said, proud that he could read every word.

Mr. Alden came over to see what Benny was talking about. "What do you know! This is the end of a trail I hiked with my own grandfather when I visited Yellowstone as a boy. We never made it this far, though. I wonder why the trails are closed."

"Maybe they're not." Henry pointed down the dirt path. "Look below. There's a backpacker climbing up this way. See? He's wearing a bright orange hat."

The Aldens peeked over the edge to see who Henry was talking about.

Mr. Alden removed his sunglasses to get a better look. "I'd like to have a chat with the fellow and find out what's going on with these trails. I'd give anything to go down a ways. I wonder if we're anywhere near the famous lost cabin."

Violet was curious, too. "What lost cabin, Grandfather?"

"Well, Violet, years ago, when I was about your age, I heard all kinds of stories

about some California gold miners," said Grandfather. "They got stuck in Yellowstone because of an early snowstorm and had to spend the winter here. The story goes that they built a log hut for themselves, but no one ever found it. There were all sorts of tales about how they may have left behind a bag of gold nuggets."

The children wanted to know more, but Mr. Alden had nothing else to share. "Maybe that hiker knows about the lost cabin," Benny whispered when the man finally reached the lookout area.

"Did you ever find the cabin, Grandfather?" Violet asked.

"I'm afraid not," Mr. Alden answered in a disappointed voice. "We never had the right maps or enough time. But looking for it was a fine summer adventure. Maybe this hiker can tell us something."

The Aldens greeted the man in the orange hat with friendly smiles.

The hiker seemed annoyed by the attention. "Tourists all over the place!" he muttered when he saw the children with their grandfather. He grew even grumpier when he had to squeeze by them to get to his truck. "This isn't a shopping mall, you know," he said to no one in particular.

Mr. Alden heard this but spoke to the man anyway. "How do you do, sir? I notice you just came up from one of the Lost Cabin Trails. But there's a sign saying they're closed. Do you have any idea why?"

The man stared at Mr. Alden, then turned away without answering.

"Sir! Sir!" Mr. Alden continued. "I'm just curious. You see, I hiked some of these trails when I was a boy. I'm hoping my grandchildren here can do the same. Is there a problem?"

This time the man stopped. "Bears everywhere," he said.

Benny shivered at the thought of bears. "But what about the lost cabin?" he asked. "The one with the gold in it."

For a few seconds, the man was silent. Finally he spoke directly to Benny. "Never was any such thing as a lost cabin. Just a lot of silly stories and fool hikers looking for something that never existed."

With that, the man threw his backpack into his pickup truck and drove off.

"That's strange," Henry said. "If the trails are closed, why was he was hiking on them? He said there were bears, but he was hiking alone, something hikers should never do around Yellowstone."

"And he wasn't wearing any bear bells, either," Jessie added. "The guidebooks say it's a good idea for hikers to wear bells or make a lot of noise to keep bears away. Bears don't like noise."

Mr. Alden put his hat back on. "That's good advice, Jessie. Well, this isn't where the Lost Cabin Trails start anyway. The trailhead is inside Yellowstone."

Benny looked disappointed. "But that hiker says there wasn't any cabin or anything."

Mr. Alden patted Benny's head. "That's one man's opinion. Some of the rest of us have a different one."

"Right," Benny said, perking up again. "They couldn't call the trails Lost Cabin Trails if there wasn't a lost cabin, right?"

Mr. Alden smiled. "Good point, Benny. Now, everyone, line up again. I'll get a picture for Mrs. McGregor."

The four children scurried back to the big log sign.

"Say cheese and crackers," Mr. Alden teased.

"Cheese and crackers," everyone said.

"And bears," Benny added, shivering just a little.

Mr. Alden snapped several pictures, then waved Benny over. "Okay, okay. Now we really can go, Benny. Hop in the car."

"Grandfather, do you really think there are any bears in Yellowstone National Park?" Benny asked.

"I don't *think* there are bears in Yellowstone, Benny, I *know* there are," Mr. Alden answered as he drove up and up the twisting mountain road. "When I was a young boy trout fishing out here, I saw a grizzly bear or two. And plenty of moose and elk and buffalo, too. You'll see some wild animals in Yellowstone, no doubt about it. But bears don't usually bother people in groups, especially noisy people. So I don't think you'll have a bear problem, Benny!"

Benny's eyes were round and bright. "Look! There's a sign that says 'Watch Out for Buffalo.' I'm watching, but I don't see any. Where are they?"

Mr. Alden chuckled. "Be patient. We're not in Yellowstone National Park just yet. First we have to stop off in the little town up ahead. It's the last good place to stock up on our hiking and fishing supplies."

"And bear bells," Benny added. "We can't forget those."

CHAPTER 2

Too Many Questions

The Aldens' car climbed even higher into the mountains leading to Yellowstone National Park. The road was narrow now, and traffic moved slowly.

"Are we almost there?" Benny asked when the Aldens' rented car got slowed down behind a big trailer.

"Not yet," Mr. Alden answered. "Just one last stop for gas and last-minute supplies. There's a general store in this town that you won't want to miss."

"If they have lunch there, then I know I

won't want to miss it!" Benny said.

The Aldens were used to hearing about Benny's appetite. No matter where he traveled or how much food the Aldens' housekeeper, Mrs. McGregor, sent along, Benny was always thinking about the next meal.

"Elkhorn's General Store hasn't changed a bit," Mr. Alden said when he spotted a large log building near the Yellowstone gates.

Mr. Alden pulled up to an old-fashioned gas pump. "Except for these gas prices, everything looks almost the same as when I was a boy. We'll get gas here."

"What I need is one of those famous ice-cream sodas you told us about, Grandfather," Benny announced.

Jessie began reading from the back of an old postcard Grandfather had given her:

"Before entering Yellowstone, be sure to stop for an ice-cream soda at Elkhorn's famous soda fountain built in 1912. Many tourists travel miles out of their way to visit this old-fashioned general store with its tiled soda fountain and swivel stools."

Inside, Elkhorn's was filled with tourists. Hikers were trying on hiking boots and backpacks. Other visitors were checking out fly-fishing rods.

Henry and Benny stood in front of a display of handy pocketknives.

A friendly white-haired man behind the counter looked at Benny. "Where are you boys going hiking?"

Benny's head barely reached the top of the counter. "How did you know we were going hiking?"

The older man's tanned, leathery face crinkled just a bit when he saw Benny waiting for an answer. "I noticed your brand-new hiking boots. And I see you have a water bottle hanging from your backpack. That's a good pack for a hike, young man. Do you need any supplies to put in it? You never want to go hiking in Yellowstone without a few things — a trail guide, a rain poncho, water, some bear bells, and — "

"Food!" Benny cried out.

"Exactly right," the man behind the counter said. "I recommend trail mix. It fills you up, and it gives you energy, too. I can make up a special batch for you."

The man stepped from behind the counter. He waved the children over to a row of bins, each one filled with nuts, dried fruit, or small candies. "Grab a bag, and I'll scoop in a few days' worth of trail mix. By the way, I'm Oz Elkhorn. I was practically born in Yellowstone National Park. Now tell me who you folks are and where you're from."

Jessie answered first. "We're the Aldens. This is my younger sister, Violet. She's ten. We're only two years apart. This is Benny, who just turned six. And that's Henry, our fourteen-year-old brother. We're from Greenfield, back east."

The man put down the scoop for a minute. "Alden? Greenfield? Hmmm. I had a boyhood friend named Jimmy Alden, younger than I am. Used to come out here with his grandfather every summer for the trout fishing. We lost touch, but I'm pretty sure he was from Greenfield. Any relation of yours?"

Benny nearly dropped his bag of trail

mix. "Our grandfather's name is Alden, too! And he lives in Greenfield! And . . . and . . ." Benny gulped some air. "And he used to come here trout fishing, and he saw grizzly bears! Only his name isn't Jimmy. It's James."

The children heard a person clearing his throat behind them. "Did I just hear my name?" Mr. Alden asked.

"Why, Jimmy Alden!" Mr. Elkhorn said, holding out his right hand. "You're white on top like me, but I know you just like yesterday."

Mr. Alden shook the older man's hand. "Ozzie Elkhorn?" he asked finally.

Mr. Elkhorn broke into a grin. "One and the same. Only I haven't been called Ozzie for quite a few years."

"And I haven't been called Jimmy since I was a boy."

"Those were good summer days, Jimmy," Oz Elkhorn said.

"The best," Mr. Alden agreed. "I've brought my four grandchildren out here so they can have some good summer days, too.

They're going to do some hiking while I go fishing. My grandchildren know all about the woods."

"We used to live in a boxcar in the woods after our parents died," Violet told Oz Elkhorn in a soft voice. "Then Grandfather found us. Now we live with him in a real house."

"But we still like the outdoors," Henry added.

"You'll get plenty of outdoors in Yellowstone," Oz Elkhorn told the children. "But first I want to outfit you with everything you need."

Benny tugged Mr. Alden's arm. "I need lunch," he whispered.

Mr. Alden laughed. "All the way through Wyoming, I told my children about this store, Oz, and your famous soda fountain. Can you still get a grilled cheese sandwich and an ice-cream soda?"

Mr. Elkhorn waved everyone to the other side of the store. "You sure can, but not for a quarter anymore."

The Aldens followed Oz to a long marble counter that stretched out before a long mirror. Old-fashioned ice-cream dishes and colored plates filled the shelves next to the mirror.

"You haven't changed much in all these years," Mr. Alden told Oz.

In no time, Oz set down five foamy chocolate ice-cream sodas in front of the Aldens. "These haven't changed, either. Give me five minutes, and you'll have grilled cheese sandwiches to go with your sodas. Now let's catch up on the last fifty years."

The Aldens finished lunch quickly. Then Mr. Alden checked his watch. "I could sit here all day talking to you, Oz, but I see how busy you are. And it's time for us to get started on our vacation."

Oz removed his white apron. "Before you leave, I want to show you Aldens some beautiful new flies I made for trout fishing," he said. "With the store so busy, I don't get much of a chance to tie many flies anymore. Still, I'd like to give you a couple of new ones I just finished. Follow me to the back of the store."

Benny looked up at Oz. "You keep flies in the back of the store? Why don't you shoo them out or try to smack them with a fly swatter?"

Oz grinned. "See these?" He pointed into a drawer under the counter in back of the store. "These are handmade flies. They look like real flies, don't they? The trout think so, anyway. We just tie them to the end of our fishing line. Then all we have to do is hope that the fish bite. The better the fly, the better the fishing."

Benny laughed. "Now I get it," he said. "They're pretend flies, not real ones."

Violet was even more interested in Oz's handmade flies than Benny was. "They're so beautiful and realistic. I can't believe you made these."

"If you get a rainy day on your vacation," Oz told Violet, "I'll teach you how to tie flies."

After giving Mr. Alden two of the flies as a present, Oz unlocked another drawer. "Here's something else that might interest you," he told the Aldens. He unrolled a yellowed sheet of paper. "It's an old hand-drawn trapper's map my granddad kept under lock and key until he died. Remember, Jimmy, how he used to bring you and your grandfather up to the Lost Cabin Trails, but he'd never let anybody see this map?"

Mr. Alden put on his reading glasses. "He drove my grandfather wild holding onto that map. Did anything special turn up after you finally got to see it?"

Oz laughed. "Believe it or not, I just got my hands on it. Granddad left a lot of old things to my cousin, who left them to me after he died last year. Lo and behold, Granddad's old trapper map was mixed in with some of my cousin's papers. I haven't had a minute to check out some of the places on the map, not even the lost cabin. See this arrow? It shows the area where the cabin might be. Some of my old guidebooks show the trails. But, far as I know, this is the only map that shows any sign of that old miner's hut."

Mr. Alden and Oz bent over the map. They couldn't stop talking about their boyhood hikes searching for the old cabin.

"You know, by the looks of this map, your grandfather steered us *away* from the lost cabin," Mr. Alden said. "The cabin seems to be toward the far end of the trails on a different branch."

Oz smiled. "Granddad had a lot of secrets. He knew about places in Yellowstone only wild animals have seen. Anyway, as far as I know, he never found the cabin, either. Otherwise, he might've died a rich man instead of a store owner."

"Tell you what," Oz said to the Aldens. "Not too many folks hike the Lost Cabin Trails anymore. They're not shown in most of the new guidebooks. How about if I make you Aldens a copy so you can go exploring? Maybe on my day off we can all go searching for the lost cabin together."

Benny looked up at Oz. "Know what?" he asked. "We met a man who said there's no cabin. He was hiking all by himself with no bear bells, either."

"Was he, now?" Oz said. "Well, I'd wonder how much a fellow hiking alone would know about lost cabins and such. Just because nobody's ever found it doesn't mean it isn't there."

Benny's face lit up when he heard this. "I bet we can find it. We have brand-new hiking boots and your map and lots of trail mix. And we're going to get bear bells, too!"

"Then you're in good shape for the Lost Cabin Trails," Oz said.

"There is one thing," Mr. Alden began. "I stopped to take a few pictures of my grandchildren in front of the Continental Divide sign — you know the one? Anyway, while we were looking around, we saw a sign that said the Lost Cabin Trails were closed."

"Nonsense!" Oz Elkhorn cried. "Parts of the trails need work — fallen-down trees and such. You just climb over them."

Mr. Alden nodded at his old friend. "I thought as much. Anyway, that hiker Benny mentioned said the trails were closed because of bear activity."

"Bear activity? Yellowstone's nothing but bear activity! This time of year, though, most of the bears are up on the other side of the park. Besides, any smart hiker knows how to keep the bears away — lots of noise and lots of companions. The chances of seeing a bear are pretty slim. There you go, Aldens." Oz handed Jessie a crisp copy of his grandfather's old map. "You kids stick together and wear some bear bells. Here's a basket of them. Take your pick."

The Aldens sorted through the basket. They selected four jingle-bell bracelets in different colors.

"What if these bells don't work?" Henry asked, trying not to sound nervous. "I mean, in case we come across a bear, what's the best thing to do?"

Oz stepped from behind the counter into the aisle. He took a few large, slow steps backward. "Step back slowly, like this. Whatever you do, don't run. Just back up slowly and make a wide turn away from the bear. With four of you, you're not likely to get into trouble with bears. Very few people ever see a single one nowadays, not like the old days. Anyway, you're all set with your bear bells, and you have a copy of my old map."

Suddenly, the Aldens heard an unfamiliar voice behind them. "Did I hear you say something about old maps? Do you sell any old maps?"

A young man in hiking clothes looked over Oz's shoulder. "All you have are some of these new guides and maps. I . . . uh . . . collect old documents. I thought an old place like this store might sell old . . . letters and . . . uh . . . you know, maps."

"Sorry, young man, I don't sell old maps. You might try the Bear's Paw Antiques down the street."

Before Oz finished his sentence, the young man was gone.

"He sure went off in a hurry, didn't he?" Oz said. "Kind of strange for a young fella like that to be interested in old stuff like maps. We sure get all kinds in here."

"Including the Alden kind," Benny said.

CHAPTER 3

Buffalo on Parade

The Aldens made several trips to their car with insect repellent, fishing gear, bottled water, hiking socks, first-aid supplies, and the very important bear bells. They were ready for the woods.

"While Grandfather pays the bill, let's thank Oz one last time," Jessie suggested after she closed the trunk.

The children strolled to the back of the store where Oz said he had some paperwork to do.

There was no sign of Oz.

Benny grabbed Jessie's arm. "Hey, look who's back there. Isn't that the hiker who told us about all the bears?"

Before Jessie could answer, the man in the orange hat looked up. He dropped the books he'd been holding and disappeared out the back door.

"What was that all about?" Henry wanted to know.

The back door opened again. This time it was Oz. He was trying to balance an armful of cardboard boxes.

"Bear bells," Oz said. "Can't keep them in stock. It's going to sound like the North Pole with all the jingling out in the woods."

"Wait, Oz!" Henry called out. He picked up the books the hiker had dropped. "There. I was afraid you were going to trip over these."

Oz carefully set the boxes down. "I guess these books must have fallen from the shelf."

"No, they didn't," Benny piped up. "That hiker man we saw ran out so fast, he dropped your books on the floor. And know what? He ran out the back door."

Oz Elkhorn laughed for a long time. "That's your mysterious hiker man? Oh, my. Well, your hiker man is Lester Crabtree. He's a summer regular, a retired fellow who works with his wife, Eleanor, at the Old Faithful Inn. He asked if he could make copies of pages in some old Yellowstone books I lent him. I just ran into him. He said he had an emergency back at the lodge. I did wonder why he went out the back door. He usually parks right out front."

"He rushed away when he saw us. He doesn't like us. Or Grandfather, either," Benny said.

Oz chuckled. "Lester Crabtree isn't the friendliest fellow. Comes out here every year with Mrs. Crabtree, who's as sweet as can be. Lester's an excellent worker but just no good with people. So the managers at the inn keep him behind the scenes — doing laundry, sweeping up, working in the kitchen — the kind of work he can do without talking much. He can be a bit of a pest, too. Always borrowing this or that old thing from me."

Jessie put her hand out to Oz. "Well, you're good with people, Mr. Elkhorn. We just wanted to thank you again for helping us out so much."

"And giving us lunch," Benny said. "Don't forget that!"

"I won't forget that. Now where's Jimmy?" Oz asked the children.

For a second Jessie was puzzled. She wasn't used to hearing her grandfather called Jimmy. "He said he'd meet us at the car."

"Well, I'll walk you out there," Oz said. "I have something special to ask him."

Mr. Alden was just getting in the car when everyone rejoined him. "Oz, I sure hope we'll get a chance to get together on your days off. If you get any, that is. We'll be at the Old Faithful Inn. Maybe you can join us for breakfast or dinner."

Oz shook Mr. Alden's hand. "No problem there. I get free meals anytime I go."

"Why's that?" Benny asked.

"I'm one of the winter keepers at the Old Faithful Inn," Oz answered.

Violet's eyes opened wide. "You keep the winter?"

Oz smiled down at Violet. "You could say that. I keep the winter away, actually. The lodge closes down at the end of October. A few of us winter keepers live there to make sure the lodge stays in tip-top shape through the winter. We can get twenty feet of snow in Yellowstone. So that's where I hibernate when the snow sets in. Getting free meals year-round is part of my pay."

"Can I work there someday?" Benny asked.

"You could probably work there now," Oz said. "Mrs. Crabtree called earlier. She asked whether I knew anyone who could give her a hand at the lodge. She needs help with odd jobs and such — housekeeping chores, carrying bags, entertaining young children while their parents have some free time — that kind of thing."

"That kind of thing is what we like to do

on our vacations!" Benny said.

"Let me give Mrs. Crabtree a call. I'll let her know you folks are available," Oz said. "Are you sure you want to spend your vacation working?"

"Working is our favorite kind of vacation," Benny said. "Do you think we'll get free meals?"

"I'll make sure you do," Oz Elkhorn answered. "Now wait right here. I'll be back in a jiffy after I speak with Mrs. Crabtree."

When Oz returned, he was grinning from ear to ear. "All set. Mrs. Crabtree wants to meet you today at five at the front desk of the lodge."

"Yippee!" Benny said.

The children waved good-bye to Oz. Just a couple of minutes later, Mr. Alden pulled into the long line of cars waiting to enter Yellowstone National Park. The line moved slowly, and Benny could hardly sit still.

Suddenly the Aldens heard a car horn blowing over and over.

"Goodness," Mr. Alden said. "There must be an emergency in the park. There's a car coming up fast on my right. I wish I could pull over, but there's no room."

No sooner had Mr. Alden finished speaking than a beat-up red car whizzed by just inches away without slowing down. The car zoomed into the park and disappeared down the road.

"The ranger let it go through without waiting in line," Henry said. "The driver must be a volunteer who has to get in the park in a hurry."

For everyone else, there was a long wait to enter Yellowstone. Finally the Aldens reached the log booth where a ranger handed Grandfather a Yellowstone map and a ticket.

"Here's your receipt, sir," the woman ranger told Mr. Alden. "Keep it near your windshield. You need it to go in and out of the park during your stay."

"Thanks," Mr. Alden said. "If I keep the receipt visible, can I avoid these long lines?"

The young woman shook her head. "Sorry, only people on official park business don't have to stop."

"What about the beat-up red car that just

flew through here?" Henry asked.

Suddenly the young woman wasn't so friendly. "What are you talking about? Now please drive on, sir. There's a long line behind you."

Mr. Alden pulled ahead. "I don't imagine that car got through without the rangers noticing. We seem to have said the wrong thing."

For a while the children were quiet. There was so much to see in the park without worrying about other cars.

"Why are we slowing down?" Benny wanted to know.

Mr. Alden pointed to a huge meadow off to the right. "There are your buffalo, Benny. A herd of them. And more crossing the road. That's what's causing this traffic jam."

Sure enough, the parade of cars, trailers, and buses had come to a complete stop. A long line of furry buffalo — big and small ones — slowly crossed the road to join the rest of the herd.

"Check the rearview mirror," Henry said. "There's a buffalo walking alongside the cars. Roll up the windows, everybody. We don't want that buffalo sticking its head in the window."

"We could practically touch it," Violet whispered when a large bushy head brushed by the Aldens' car. "Not that I would."

The Aldens sat back and enjoyed the buffalo parade.

That's when Henry noticed the red car about ten cars ahead. "Ha! That old red car is stuck here, just like us."

Mr. Alden tapped on the steering wheel. "Never pays to race around just to gain a few minutes."

Soon the herd of buffalo was out of the road. Traffic began to move again.

"We're almost there," Henry said, turning around to his brother and sisters. "The Old Faithful Inn is the next turn."

"Hey, look!" Benny cried. "There's the Old Faithful geyser."

Sure enough, off in the distance, a tower of steam shot through the air. The geyser seemed nearly as tall as the huge Old Faithful Inn several hundred yards away.

"Can you drive faster, Grandfather?" Benny asked. "I want to see the geyser up close."

Mr. Alden laughed. "Not to worry. Old Faithful goes off about every seventy minutes or so around the clock. Our rooms overlook the geyser. You'll see it dozens of times during our stay."

In five minutes the geyser had disappeared, but the Old Faithful Inn had not. The log building, several stories high, with porches halfway around, stood directly in front of the Aldens.

"Wow!" Henry said. "The Old Faithful Inn is some log cabin!"

And so it was. When the Aldens entered the inn's huge lobby with their luggage, they couldn't stop looking up, down, and all around. The lobby was buzzing with guests enjoying the amazing log room with its stone fireplace, nearly three stories high. Young children ran around the balconies that overlooked the lobby. Older people sat on oversized log chairs and couches and enjoyed the view below.

After registering, Mr. Alden led his

grandchildren up two flights of a staircase made of twisted logs several feet thick. "Your room is on the top floor."

"Wow!" Benny said when they reached the third-floor balcony. "We can see everything and everybody from this balcony. This is a good spying place."

Mr. Alden laughed. "I hope you don't have to do any spying this vacation. You've already filled your schedule with your jobs here."

Benny looked over the balcony railing. "Hey, isn't that the man we saw at Oz's store? The one who wanted old maps? What's he doing straightening chairs in front of the fireplace?"

The other children came over for a look. Sure enough, down below was the very same young man the children had seen a few hours before.

"He's wearing a uniform," Jessie noticed. "He must work here."

Violet squinted down at the young man. "I wonder if we'll be working with him."

Mr. Alden checked his watch. "You'll

soon find out. Oz said you should meet with Mrs. Crabtree in about half an hour. You kids put your bags in your room, and I'll put mine into my room. Then we can stroll around the inn."

When they met in the hallway, Henry pointed out a window.

"Hey, people are lining up out there for the geyser," he said. "I guess it's like a movie or a show."

"Only no tickets," Benny said.

Mr. Alden headed down the stairs. "I'm going down to the Activities Desk to check on some overnight fishing trips. Oz mentioned a tour bus that leaves every morning for the other side of the park. The fishing is supposed to be pretty good up that way. Just one small reminder. You'll have to be extra quiet in your room. These old wooden walls are pretty thin — no insulation. You can hear every little sound."

"Goody!" Benny said. "I like that. But don't worry, Grandfather, I'll only be noisy in the woods to keep the bears away."

CHAPTER 4

Something Is Missing

The Aldens were supposed to start unpacking, but that would just have to wait. Old Faithful, the most famous geyser in the world, was about to perform again.

"Look at all the people hurrying so they won't miss it," Violet said, leaning against the windowsill.

Benny knelt on a chair to get a better view. "Can we go outside and see it up close?"

"Sure thing," Henry said.

In no time, the Aldens joined the stream

of tourists heading for the geyser. They found a place at the edge of the walkway that circled the geyser area.

"Wow!" Benny said a few seconds later when a huge plume of steam rose in the air.

A whooshing sound, like the biggest hot shower in the world, muffled the crowd's cheering and clapping. Then, a few minutes later, everyone quieted down. The plume of steam grew smaller. When the steam disappeared back into the ground, the crowd clapped and cheered again.

Henry laughed. "It *is* quite a show."

"What makes a geyser, anyway?" Benny asked. "And all the other steamy things coming out of the ground in Yellowstone?"

As usual, Jessie knew the answer. "The ground around here has lots of cracks that go down into the earth for miles. When rain and snow fall down the cracks, the cold water hits all the hot liquid inside the earth. That makes the steam blow up into the air. I read that the Old Faithful Inn once tried to run a pipe of steam from a small geyser up in the hills to the inn."

Benny got all excited when he heard this. "You mean we could take a geyser shower?"

Jessie laughed. "The system didn't really work. The geyser dried up. Geysers are very delicate. That's why there are signs all over telling people not to throw anything into them."

"I would never do that," Benny said. "I guess I'll have to take plain old showers, not geyser showers."

"Just think," Jessie said as they walked back to their room, "in seventy minutes or so, the Old Faithful geyser will start up all over again. In the meantime, I guess we'd better head back to our room to unpack before we meet with Mrs. Crabtree."

Unpacking took the Aldens no time at all, since they were such experienced travelers. In just a few minutes, all their vacation clothes were folded in drawers or hung on pegs.

Jessie lined up everyone's hiking supplies on the dresser. "I'm putting our guidebooks, Oz's map, our sunglasses, and our empty water bottles on this dresser by the door. We'll want to get a fast start in the morning and not leave anything behind."

Henry checked his watch. "I wish there was time for a quick shower."

"I wish there were towels for a quick shower," Jessie said, looking high and low for washcloths and towels.

While she was searching, someone knocked at the door.

"Who's there?" Henry asked.

"Housekeeping," a man's voice answered. "Sorry, the staff delivered your towels to the wrong room."

Henry unlocked the door. "Just what we were looking — " Henry stopped talking. "Oh, it's . . . uh . . ."

The other children came to the door to see who was there. Standing in the doorway was Mr. Crabtree, the hiker with the orange hat. Only now he wasn't wearing his hiking hat or his backpack or his hiking boots. Instead, he had on an Old Faithful Inn uniform and an identification badge.

Mr. Crabtree seemed just as surprised to see the Aldens — and none too pleased, either. "Here," he said, standing there with a stack of white towels.

Henry held out his arms for the towels. "Thanks, Mr. Crabtree. We're the Aldens. We met this morning, up near the Continental Divide, remember?"

"Don't forget to mention Oz's store," Benny whispered to Henry.

"And we saw you at Elkhorn's General Store, too." Henry moved closer to take the towels, but Mr. Crabtree held on to them. "I'm Henry Alden, and these are my sisters, Jessie and Violet, and my brother, Benny. We're friends of Oz's, too. He told us your name."

Mr. Crabtree ignored Henry's introductions. "Here are your towels. They get changed every couple of days. If you need more, call Housekeeping."

With that, Mr. Crabtree put the towels on a small space on the dresser. The stack of towels was so tall, it toppled over, knocking several items off the dresser.

"This is where we usually deliver the towels," Mr. Crabtree said sharply. "If you clutter up the space, there's no room."

Benny whispered to Violet, "He just picked up Oz's map."

Sure enough, Mr. Crabtree clutched Oz's map in his hand along with a water bottle and some suntan lotion that had slipped off the dresser. When he realized all four children were staring at him, Mr. Crabtree put everything back in a jumble. Without another word, he left the room.

"Oz was right," Jessie began. "Mr. Crabtree sure isn't too friendly to the guests. Maybe he was hoping nobody would be here."

"You're right, Jessie," said Henry. "It looked as if he was after the map. If we hadn't been here, he could have easily picked it up."

At five o'clock sharp, the Aldens reported to the front desk of the Old Faithful Inn. Long lines of people were waiting to register. Others stood in line waiting for the inn's beautiful old dining room to open for dinner.

The Aldens looked around the bustling lobby. The lodge was such a busy place.

"I bet there are all kinds of jobs we can do here," Jessie said. "There's so much going on."

At that moment, an older woman with curly gray hair came over to the children. "Are you the Aldens?" she asked, a bit out of breath. "I'm Eleanor Crabtree. Sorry I'm a little late, but we're short of help. I got behind on my work."

Henry shook the woman's hand. "We're the Aldens—Jessie, Violet, Benny, and I'm Henry. Glad to meet you."

The woman took a deep breath. "And am I ever glad to meet you! We're shorthanded this week. I just finished straightening out a problem with our towel deliveries."

"Our towels went to another room," Violet said. "But your husband, Mr. Crabtree, dropped them off right before we came down here."

Mrs. Crabtree look relieved and seemed to relax. "I'm so glad to hear that. So I guess you met Lester. He likes to keep to himself.

Usually he stays behind the scenes in the kitchen or the laundry room. But today I had to give the staff some extra chores."

"Mr. Elkhorn told us you need some extra people to fill in for some college students," Jessie said. "I hope we can help. We've worked in lots of places before."

Mrs. Crabtree smiled at the children. "Well, if you can start right now, I'd love you to supervise some young children for about an hour. We offer baby-sitting to parents so they can have a nice, quiet dinner in our dining room."

"We like taking care of children," Jessie said.

"Because we are children," Benny added, "we know what they like — games and stories and solving mysteries."

Mrs. Crabtree had to laugh. "Then I know Oz Elkhorn sent me the right helpers. I don't know about solving mysteries, but you've solved a lot of problems just by showing up. Anyway, there are about six children you can look after."

Mrs. Crabtree pointed up to the first-story balcony. "See those parents and children up in the corner? Well, one of my other workers, a college student named Sam Jackson, is up there with them. Now that all of you are here, you can stay with the children while their parents go to dinner. I need Sam to tidy up some of the rooms instead. Just follow me."

As the children climbed the log staircase to the balcony, Mrs. Crabtree explained where everything was and what to do. "There's a cabinet full of art supplies, books, games, and some toys. The children can draw or listen to stories or play games. And don't forget our geyser. That's our biggest entertainment. It goes off in a little while."

"May we take the children outdoors to see it?" Jessie wanted to know.

"Absolutely," Mrs. Crabtree answered. "You can view it from the porch just outside the balcony area."

The children followed Mrs. Crabtree to the corner of the first balcony. That's when the Aldens recognized a familiar face.

"*Psst*, Jessie," Henry whispered. "Isn't that the fellow who asked Oz about old maps at the store today?"

"Sam," Mrs. Crabtree said, waving to the young man. "Come over and meet the Aldens. They're going to take over the children's hour for now. I need you for room cleaning—emptying trash and such. We're dreadfully behind."

"We already met this morning," Jessie said, smiling at the young man.

Sam Jackson looked away.

"At Elkhorn's?" Henry reminded Sam. "We were in back of the store with Mr. Elkhorn. He was copying something for us."

Now Mrs. Crabtree looked confused. "You went to Elkhorn's this morning, Sam? I thought you just picked up supplies at the depot down the road. I wondered why you were gone so long when I needed you here."

Looking at the Aldens, Sam tightened his lips. "I . . . uh . . . had to pick up a spare part for my car. Anyway, the important thing is that I came back in time for the children's hour. Here I am. I was just about to read the kids a story. Afterward I'm going to take them out to the porch to watch the geyser."

Mrs. Crabtree checked her clipboard. "Well, plans have changed a bit. This is a perfect job for the Aldens right now since I haven't the time to show them around. They can do housekeeping and deliveries another day when they're more familiar with the lodge."

Sam Jackson looked upset with this change of plans.

"Don't worry, Sam," Mrs. Crabtree went on. "I'll post you back here again. Now please be down in the laundry area in ten minutes to pick up the room keys and a cleaning cart. In the meantime, why don't you introduce the children to the Aldens."

After Mrs. Crabtree left, the Aldens waited for Sam to say something. At first he didn't move or speak. Some of the smaller children began to look worried.

"I want my mommy and daddy," a small

boy said. "They're down there having dinner. I want to see them."

Violet bent down to make the little boy feel better. "There, there. You know what? Before we see your mommy and daddy, we're going to read you a story. Then we'll go see the geyser."

"I saw the geyser already," a little girl said, twisting the end of her pigtail around her finger. "I want to see my mommy and daddy, too, not the geyser."

Jessie came over to the little girl. "I'm Jessie. Can I guess your name? Is it . . . Tiddledeedo?"

The little girl gave a tiny smile and shook her head.

"Is it Mousymiss? Or Sunnypup?"

"Her name is Becky," Sam Jackson said sharply. "They don't have silly names like that. That's Davy, Lauren, Scotty, Emily, and Katy."

The little girl named Katy looked up at Sam Jackson. "How come you can't play a game like you said?"

The Aldens looked at Sam Jackson. He

took a long time answering, this time in a softer voice. "Sorry, Katy. Mrs. Crabtree doesn't want me here anymore. I have to go clean rooms. These other people will play a game with you, okay? I've got to leave now."

"Oh, look," Jessie said before Sam left. She picked up a book lying on top of the bookcase. "Here's a book called *The Tale of the Lost Cabin Miners*. Would you children like me to read that to you? Did you know there's a lost cabin way up in the mountains of Yellowstone?"

"And we're going to find it!" Benny told the excited children.

Sam Jackson walked over to Jessie. "That book doesn't belong here. Somebody must have left it here by mistake. I'll put it in the Lost and Found box."

Sam held his hand out.

Jessie looked at the book and gave it to Sam. "Here," she said softly. "I wouldn't want to take a book that belongs to someone else."

Sam grabbed the book, turned, then disappeared down the steps.

"Is Sam coming back?" the little boy named Davy asked.

"He'll be back another day," Violet said as she set up the gameboard and pieces Sam had taken out for the children. "Now, who wants to play a game with Benny and me?"

"We do!" four of the children said.

Now that the Aldens were there to keep them busy, the children didn't have too much time to think about missing Sam or their parents.

The other children squeezed themselves between Jessie and Henry on one of the inn's long cozy couches. Jessie began to read a story about a moose named Mike and an elk named Elkie who lived together in Yellowstone but couldn't get along.

The hour flew by. The Aldens took the children out to the porch overlooking the geyser area. After Old Faithful went off, the children's parents came back for them.

"Can you play with us tomorrow?" little Davy asked Violet. "And the day after that, too?"

"I hope so," Violet answered.

The redheaded girl named Lauren pulled on Jessie's sleeve. "Where are you going with your brothers and sister?"

Jessie smiled. "Back to our room to change. Then we're going to meet our grandfather in the dining room and have a great big dinner."

The parents of the little ones thanked the Aldens.

"That was fun," Violet said as she and her brothers and sister strolled down the dim hallways that led to their room. "I hope we do that job every night — I mean if Sam Jackson is busy."

Benny looked up at Violet. "Know what? That was fun, but I'm hungry. I wish we could eat when the parents eat."

The older children laughed.

"Then we wouldn't be able to work," Jessie said. "Our jobs come first, then our dinner."

Henry unlocked the door. The room was cleaner than they'd left it. Even their suitcases and hiking boots were lined up in neat rows.

"I guess somebody from Housekeeping came by again," Jessie said, picking up two pieces of paper lying on the bed. "Oh, somebody dropped off our job schedule. It looks as if we have to be at the laundry area tomorrow afternoon. That gives us time for a morning hike. I'm glad Mrs. Crabtree sent over this floor map, too. The lodge is so big, it would be easy to get lost."

"Jessie," Henry said in a quiet, serious voice. "Speaking of maps, have you seen our copy of Oz's map?"

"It was right on the corner of the dresser when we left," Jessie told Henry.

Henry checked under the dresser, then under the bed. "Well, it's not here now."

The children searched high and low one more time. But Henry was right. The copy of the Lost Cabin Trails map had vanished.

"You don't think Mr. Crabtree would have taken it, do you?" asked Jessie.

"I don't know, Jessie," said Henry. "I don't know."

CHAPTER 5

Lost in the Woods

The Aldens didn't need an alarm clock at the Old Faithful Inn the next day.

Henry pulled the covers over his head. "What's that spotlight?" he said with a groan.

Benny hopped out of bed, and pulled back the curtains. "It's the geyser. Neat!"

Jessie and Violet crawled out of bed. Sure enough, Old Faithful was faithfully shooting steam into the air. Each time the geyser shot up, it blocked the rising sun like a shadow.

Violet leaned on her elbows to watch the geyser. "It's awfully pretty in the morning with the sun coming up and all," she said.

After the geyser gurgled back into the ground, the rising sun shone steadily.

"I smell bacon," Benny announced soon afterward.

"First the geyser, now bacon," Henry said. "I guess it's time to get up."

The children took turns taking hot showers and climbing into their hiking clothes.

Jessie checked under the bed one more time for the missing copy of Oz's map. "I sure wanted to hike the Lost Cabin Trails today. I guess we can do some of the other hikes instead."

"Look," Benny said in an excited voice. "I tied my hiking boots by myself."

"Shhh." Jessie put her finger to her lips. "Remember what Grandfather said. The walls are thin. We don't want to wake up the whole lodge."

Quietly, the children filled their water bottles and backpacks with everything they would need on their hike. They were so quiet, they could hear some people whispering in the hallway.

"Just stay away from them, that's all I can tell you," a woman's voice said. "If anyone finds out, our whole plan will fall apart."

Benny put his ear near the keyhole. He heard footsteps fading away. He opened the door, but no one was there.

"Good morning, Aldens!" Mrs. Crabtree said when the children arrived in the dining room awhile later. "Your grandfather is sitting over by the fireplace. I'll meet you this afternoon — at three in the laundry area, then at five up on the balcony. The children loved you last night. They requested more Aldens tonight. Have a wonderful breakfast."

The children joined their grandfather. He was dressed for his fishing trip.

"Well, I'm ready for a couple of days of fishing," Grandfather Alden said, putting down his cup of coffee. "And the four of you look all set for your hike on the Lost

Cabin Trails." Then he noticed his grand-children's disappointed faces. "Oh, my. Did I say the wrong thing?"

"Oz's map disappeared," Jessie explained. "I thought we put it on the dresser next to our hiking gear. When we came back last night, we couldn't find it. We'll have to go hiking someplace else until we get another copy."

Mr. Alden put down his coffee cup. "Not to worry. I received a phone message from Oz last night. He'll be arriving here in about an hour. I have just enough time to give him a call right now. I'm sure he can make another copy of the map and bring it along."

The children placed their breakfast or-ders after Mr. Alden left to call Oz. While they waited for their food to arrive, they spotted Sam Jackson cleaning tables nearby. When Sam looked up, the children waved, but he turned away.

"Why doesn't Sam like us?" Benny asked.

Violet looked thoughtful. "Maybe he likes taking care of the children instead of picking up dirty dishes or cleaning rooms."

The other children thought about Violet's comment. They wanted to work with Sam, but he didn't want to work with them.

The children's meals soon arrived, and they began eating.

Mr. Alden looked upset when he returned. "There may have been a theft at Elkhorn's," he told his grandchildren. "When I asked Oz whether he could make another copy of his grandfather's old trail map, he told me he's been looking for it since yesterday. He still hasn't found it. He's bringing you one of his old guidebooks that shows the trails."

Henry took a deep breath. "There's something about that map."

At that very moment, everyone heard a crash nearby. Sam Jackson had dropped a tray of silverware right next to the table where the Aldens were sitting.

Henry leaned down to help Sam.

Sam shooed Henry away. "I'll clean up this mess," he said. "This is my job. You have my other job. Isn't that enough?"

"Sorry," Henry said. "I just wanted to help."

Sam turned his back on Henry without another word.

A short while later, the Aldens passed Sam on their way out of the dining room. He was eating his breakfast now, in the small snack bar next to the big dining room. And he wasn't alone. He was with a young woman in a ranger uniform.

"Isn't that the ranger we saw at the Yellowstone gates when we arrived?" Jessie asked Henry. "The one who said nobody could go into the park without stopping at the gate?"

Henry took another look. "Could be."

Benny pulled on Henry's arm. "Do you think they were talking in the hallway this morning outside our room?"

Before Henry could answer, Benny noticed someone else. "Oh, look who else is here."

Oz Elkhorn was standing by the registration desk and chatting with Mrs. Crabtree. Map or no map, he was pleased to see the Aldens.

"Hello there," he said. "What a morning!

First Granddad's map is missing. Then I got caught behind a trailer coming up the mountains. Anyway, I found something for you. It's an old guidebook with most of the Lost Cabin Trails on it. The cabin isn't marked on it, but at least you have something to get you started."

Oz waved the children over to the window where the light was brighter. He opened a worn-looking hiking book. "See, here's where the trail starts, not too far from the lodge. Now, if I'm not mistaken, Granddad's map showed the lost cabin to be up this way, going south. You could take a look around, anyway. Maybe our maps will turn up in the next day or so."

The children studied the guidebook.

"Well, let's go," Jessie said.

Grandfather looked over Henry's shoulder. "After I leave, why don't you ask that ranger whether the trails are open. Now let's have some hugs. The tour bus for my fishing trip is about to depart. I'll see you after a couple of days of fishing."

The children lined up for good-bye hugs.

"So long, children. So long, Oz," Mr. Alden said. "Oz, will you do a last-minute check before my children head out hiking?"

Oz turned to the children. "Sure thing. Let's see. Water bottles?"

"Check," the children answered.

"First aid?"

"Check."

"Trail mix?"

"Check."

"Rain ponchos?"

"Check."

"Guidebooks, compass, binoculars?"

"Check. Check. Check."

Oz put his hand on Benny's shoulder. "Then head for the hills, young man."

Benny looked up. He had a question, too. "You forgot to ask us if we have one other thing."

Oz was curious. "What is that?"

"Bear bells!" Benny cried. He shook his wrist so the bear bells jingled.

"Check!" Oz said.

CHAPTER 6

Mud Pots and Other Oddities

When the Aldens set out for the Lost Cabin trailhead, they noticed a ranger heading toward the Visitors' Center.

"Hey, let's ask that ranger if the trails are open," Henry suggested. He tapped the ranger on the shoulder. "Oh, hi," he said timidly to the young woman, when he realized who she was.

"You gave us our tickets at the gate when we arrived in Yellowstone," Jessie said to the ranger when she caught up to Henry. "You probably don't remember us since you see so many people. We have a question about a hike we want to take this morning."

"Well, what is it?" the young woman asked.

Henry took Oz's guidebook from his jacket pocket. "We want to hike these trails," he said, showing the young woman the map in the guidebook. "They're the Lost Cabin Trails, but we want to make sure they're open. Yesterday we saw a sign saying they were closed."

The woman's hand shook slightly when she picked up Oz's guidebook. "If you saw a sign, that means those trails are closed. Now I really must go," she said, leaving the Aldens on the path.

The children stood there and tried to get the young woman's attention again.

"Ranger Crowe!" Jessie called out after remembering the name on the young woman's name badge. "Would you just tell us why the trails are closed?"

Ranger Crowe kept right on walking. Finally, without turning around, she yelled out an answer. "Too many fallen trees."

Benny sadly took off his bear bells and stuck them in his backpack.

Jessie put her arm around Benny. "Now, now. Let's at least check the trailhead. It's just across that log bridge. I'll go check."

Jessie crossed the bridge. A second later she waved. "Come on over," she yelled across the bridge. "The trail looks open on this end."

A few minutes later, all of the Aldens stood before the faded trailhead sign for the Lost Cabin Trails.

Henry checked Oz's guidebook. "This says the trails run eight miles altogether. We have time to go halfway. We have to be back for our jobs by three o'clock. Ready?"

Everybody but Benny was ready. He was searching for something in his backpack. "Oh, here it is. My trail mix. Just a teeny bit—for energy."

Jessie laughed. "Goodness, Benny, we just started out. Make sure to save some for lunch at the top of the mountain."

The children were quiet as they made their way up the trail. On the lower slopes, some of the trees were just tall bare black stumps. All their needles and branches had burned in Yellowstone's big fires a few years before.

Jessie pointed out dozens of small pine trees growing in some grassy areas right under the burned trees. "These are baby pine trees. After the Yellowstone fires, the pinecones popped open and seeds dropped to the ground. That's where these little trees came from. Wildfires can help start new forests."

In a short time, the children left the area of burned trees. Ahead was a green, woodsy trail. The trail got steeper, so the children were quiet. They saved their breath for climbing.

About an hour later, they reached the mountaintop. The wind was blowing hard now. The children huddled together for warmth.

"Whew, look how far up we are," Henry said, rubbing his arms.

Benny pointed to a log building way down below. "Hey, is that the lost cabin down there?"

The other three children laughed.

"That's the Old Faithful Inn, Benny," Violet said. "But you're right. It does look like a small log cabin from way up here."

"Nuts," Benny said. Then he wriggled out of his backpack straps. "Nuts remind me of my trail mix."

The other children sat down to enjoy their trail mix, too.

"Drink plenty of water," Jessie advised when Henry went off to check some of the other trails. "Then we'll have energy for hiking back down. First I have to check Oz's guidebook. I'd like to take a different trail on our way back."

"Goody!" Benny said. "Maybe we'll see the cabin if we go a different way."

Henry gave Benny's shoulder a friendly squeeze when he returned and overheard this. "I was thinking the same thing. Anyway, I noticed some hikers placed stone markers along one of the other trails. Those will help us out."

The Aldens gathered up their packs. They began to hike on a new trail. Going down was tricky. They took careful steps, rock by rock, turn by turn.

"What's that creaking—" Jessie asked before a loud crash drowned out her voice.

The children looked uphill. A large pine branch had fallen just yards away from where they had been hiking.

Henry studied Jessie's face without saying anything. They were thinking the same thing. The wind was picking up. More branches fell around them. They needed to get back to the lodge soon.

"Let's speed it up, guys, okay?" Henry said. "It's a little too windy to be out hiking."

After a while, the children were relieved to reach a sheltered sandy area. They heard a strange sound coming from underground.

"What's that?" Benny asked. "It sounds like Mrs. McGregor's washing machine."

Sure enough, the gurgling and slurping sounded just like a washing machine at slow speed.

"Mud pots!" Jessie said in an excited voice. "They're holes in the ground with hot, bubbling mud inside."

When the Aldens drew closer to the sound, they saw several holes of steaming grayish mud boiling like a pot of Mrs. McGregor's stew.

Jessie put her arm in front of Benny and Violet. "Stand way back here behind the barrier. I don't want us to wind up taking a mud bath."

"Me neither," Benny said, but he was excited by the idea of a bubbling hot mud bath.

Henry noticed Jessie checking the old guidebook again. "What's the matter, Jessie? Is anything wrong?"

Jessie looked up, her eyebrows wrinkled in worry. "These mud pots shouldn't be here. I mean, we shouldn't be here. The guidebook shows that the trails going back to the lodge aren't anywhere near these mud pots. We're heading *away* from the lodge."

"Oh, no," Henry said, trying to keep his voice calm. "Those signs at the top and the trail markers pointed the wrong way."

Violet looked up at Henry. "Does that mean we have to hike back up again? There are so many branches falling."

"The best thing to do is climb to the top again," Henry said. "Then we'll take the same trail down that we hiked up. Now let's have some more water and trail mix. That'll give us plenty of energy. But save a little, too."

The Aldens started the long climb back up the mountain without saying much. Violet decided to enjoy the sight of the chattering ground squirrels and the colorful wildflowers that grew everywhere.

Soon Henry noticed birds by a rushing brook. "Look," he said. "It's a couple of dipper birds."

Soon, all the children were laughing at two silly gray birds dunking their heads over and over into the stream. For a few minutes, the children forgot about the winds blowing everything around and that they still had a long climb ahead.

The children took deep breaths and began their upward hike again. A half hour later, they reached the top of the mountain.

"Should we have lunch again?" Benny asked.

Jessie and Henry looked at each other and shook their heads.

Jessie took Benny's hand. "Let's save room for something at the snack bar. But here's a sip of water from my bottle. Take some, too, Violet."

"Okay," Benny and Violet said.

This time Henry and Jessie followed the guidebook trail exactly. No detours.

After a long while, the wind died down. The children even heard a friendly sound. Bear bells.

"More hikers," Jessie said in a happy voice.

"I like seeing other hikers, too," Henry confessed. "That means we're getting closer to the lodge." He looked through his binoculars to see if the Old Faithful Inn was anywhere in view. "Hey, look at this, Jessie," he said, handing his sister the binoculars. "Doesn't that look like Sam Jackson down on the lower part of the trail? He's sitting down there talking with Ranger Crowe."

Jessie focused the binoculars. "It sure does. Let's go down there. Maybe we can all hike back together. I'd like to get to know them better."

"I hope Sam is friendlier when he's hiking instead of working," Benny said hopefully. "I can offer him some of my trail mix."

But Benny never got a chance to offer Sam his trail mix. As soon as Ranger Crowe spotted the Aldens, she stood up from the rock where she and Sam had been sitting.

"Don't stop here," she said to the children. "The trails are dangerous with all this wind. It's not safe to be hiking here right now. Please keep moving."

Henry stopped anyway. "But it's not windy anymore. Anyway, Sam, would you like to hike back with us?"

Sam Jackson looked at Ranger Crowe, then back at the Aldens. "I'm not by myself. I had a little time off. So I'm . . . uh . . . helping Ranger Crowe clear some fallen branches off the trails."

Benny was frozen to the spot. "Hey, what about that other trail, Jessie?" Benny pointed to a path behind the rock where

Sam and Ranger Crowe had been sitting. "Maybe it's a shortcut."

Ranger Crowe blocked the path Benny was talking about. "This isn't a trail. It just goes in a few feet. You have to stay on this main trail. Sam is helping me clear everyone out of here. Please move along."

The Aldens didn't have any choice. If a park ranger said the trails were dangerous, they'd better get going.

After they had left Sam and Ranger Crowe, the Aldens slowed down a little when they reached a clearing.

Shortly, the children reached the Old Faithful geyser viewing area. Crowds of people filled the benches and walkways. The lodge porch was packed with geyser watchers, too.

But one person wasn't watching the geyser at all. Up on the porch stood someone who had been watching the Aldens ever since they came off the trails.

CHAPTER 7

Lost and Found

At three o'clock sharp, the Aldens reported to the lodge's laundry room. The huge, warm room was filled with swooshing sounds and soapy smells.

"I hear a gurgling sound again," Benny said. "Only this time, it really is washing machines, not mud pots."

"Mud pots?" Mrs. Crabtree said when she overheard the Aldens. "Did you go to the Chocolate Pots up over by Gibbon Meadow this morning? I thought for sure you children would be up on the trails breaking in your new hiking boots."

"We did see mud pots, but not the Chocolate Pots," Jessie said. "There are some others near the Lost Cabin Trails. That's where we were."

Mrs. Crabtree put her finger to her lips. "Shhh. I hope my husband isn't around to hear you say that. He likes to think those are his own private trails. Every summer he spends all the free time he has searching for some silly treasure."

Now Benny Alden was a boy who thought treasures were serious business. "But it's not a silly treasure," he said. "It's gold nuggets! And they might be hidden in a cabin. Only the cabin is hidden, too. Nobody can find it—except us, maybe."

Mrs. Crabtree patted Benny's head. "You know, the more I think about it, the more I think you children should be out having fun. This is your vacation time. You should be searching for lost cabins and gold nuggets, not working in this busy lodge."

Henry checked the schedule book lying open on Mrs. Crabtree's desk. "But working at the lodge is fun, too. It's like being backstage in a play. We get to be guests and workers at the same time. When I go to college someday, I want to spend my summers working here, just like Sam Jackson."

Mrs. Crabtree sighed. "Ah, yes, Sam. I wish he'd been placed in one of our outdoor programs, not in the lodge. He spends all his free time, and some work time, too, with one of the rangers. Unfortunately, I need him in here, not outside. Anyway, I sent him to town this morning on an errand."

The Aldens looked at each other. They said nothing. It was up to Sam to explain why he had been on the Lost Cabin Trails that morning and not running errands in town.

"Well, since Sam isn't here, what chores can we do?" Jessie asked.

Mrs. Crabtree checked her schedule book. "If you don't mind getting a little dusty, there's some room cleaning to do. A tour bus just left, and another one is coming in two hours. It would be a huge help to my staff if you could empty the waste-baskets and vacuum each of the rooms the tour bus guests were in," Mrs. Crabtree said. "That will give the regular staff more time to do everything else. Take one of those cleaning carts over there and a vacuum cleaner. Here's a list of the rooms that need immediate attention. Oh, and here are some smocks so you don't get dusty."

Jessie buttoned up her smock. "Okay, troops. All set?"

"All set," Henry said. He turned to Mrs. Crabtree. "We'll make sure to be done by five o'clock. We want to be ready to baby-sit the guests' children."

Mrs. Crabtree nodded. "Thank you for reminding me. Oh, and I'll have Sam join you. Tonight twelve children are signed up, so I need lots of helpers. Sam said he'd be back from town by then. In fact, I expected to see him a lot sooner."

"Back from town?" Jessie whispered to Henry after Mrs. Crabtree left. "Sam was on the trails with Ranger Crowe. I wonder whether he changed his plans."

"Or maybe his plans are to change his *story*," Henry replied.

The Aldens pushed their cleaning cart and dragged along the vacuum cleaner to the hall where most of the tour bus guests had been staying. Room by room, they went down the hall, vacuuming and emptying trash into a big barrel on the cart before moving on.

"This barrel is full," Henry said after they finished cleaning several rooms. "Let's take it to one of the Dumpsters in the laundry area. There's a freight elevator at the end of this hall that goes downstairs."

When the Aldens arrived in the laundry room, Mr. and Mrs. Crabtree were there.

"Now, Lester, don't tell me you were out hiking alone this morning," Mrs. Crabtree was telling her husband. "It's too dangerous to be out on those trails by yourself."

"Hi, Mrs. Crabtree," Henry said. "Hi, Mr. Crabtree. We need to empty this barrel so we can finish cleaning up the last few rooms."

Mrs. Crabtree seemed relieved to see the children. "Lester," she said, turning to her husband again, "if you want help finding that silly treasure, bring the Aldens along. Then you'll have four extra sets of eyes and some extra voices to keep the bears away. Truly, it worries me so when you hike alone."

"Nonsense, Eleanor," Mr. Crabtree said. "I never get far from the parking lot. Now let me take that barrel from you kids," he said to the Aldens. "Otherwise Eleanor will have me baby-sitting or entertaining the guests, and I'll get fired."

The Aldens looked at Mrs. Crabtree. She was the boss.

"Fine, Lester. You can finish the Aldens' cleanup chores," she told her husband.

The Aldens carried the barrel to one of the Dumpsters just outside the laundry room. Jessie opened the side door of the Dumpster for Henry.

Before Henry had lifted the trash barrel, Jessie noticed a familiar piece of paper. She pulled it from the top of the trash. "Wait, Henry! Look what I found."

"Our copy of Oz's lost cabin map!" Violet cried. "Why is it in the trash?"

At that moment, Mr. Crabtree came in. "What are you kids up to? You're not picking through the trash, are you? Shut the Dumpster. We don't want to attract field mice."

Henry banged the door shut. "Sorry. It's just that we found something we were looking for."

When the children turned around, Mr. Crabtree had taken the barrel and dumped it in a second Dumpster.

"Mr. Crabtree! Mr. Crabtree!" Jessie waved her copy of Oz's map. "Do you know anything about this?"

Mr. Crabtree didn't even turn around. He simply took the barrel and boarded the freight elevator. Before the Aldens could catch up, the doors closed, and Mr. Crabtree was gone.

"He sure was acting strange," Violet said.

"But at least we found our copy of the map," Jessie said.

CHAPTER 8

Hidden Voices

When the children returned to the laundry room, Sam Jackson had arrived for work.

Mrs. Crabtree was scolding Sam. "I'm pleased you were able to pick up the shipment of new towels, Sam. But I expected you back sooner. Was there a lot of traffic on the mountain roads?"

Sam looked at the Aldens, then down at his muddy hiking boots. "Kind of," he answered. "I'm sorry. I'll work later tonight in the dining room."

For a second Mrs. Crabtree said nothing. Then she took a deep breath. "I needed you this afternoon more than I will tonight. After guests check out, we only have a few hours to clean the rooms before the next guests arrive. Thank goodness I had the Aldens here — and my husband — to finish the housekeeping chores."

Now Sam perked up. "But I did a good job cleaning the rooms yesterday, didn't I?"

Mrs. Crabtree sighed again. "Of course you did, Sam. You're efficient when you're here. But you're often gone or late. Or something. In any case, every day at the lodge is a new one — new guests, new rooms to clean. Yesterday's work starts all over again."

"I'm sorry," Sam repeated. "I'll try to be around more."

Mrs. Crabtree checked her schedule book again. "All right, then. In an hour I'd like you to meet the Aldens upstairs for the children's hour. We have twelve children signed up this evening—six more than last night."

Sam looked at the Aldens, then back at

Mrs. Crabtree. "I can handle twelve as easily as six."

But Mrs. Crabtree was firm. "No, Sam. You'll need the Aldens, too. Some of the children asked for them as well as you. That's final."

Sam and the Aldens left the laundry room together, but they didn't stay together. As soon as he was out of Mrs. Crabtree's sight, Sam left the building.

"Should we have told Mrs. Crabtree about seeing Sam on the Lost Cabin Trails?" Violet asked.

"The important thing is that Sam brought Mrs. Crabtree the towels she needed from town," Jessie said. "Maybe Sam just decided to help out Ranger Crowe on the way back. I guess it's not our business that he also went hiking."

Henry looked very serious. "There is something that is our business."

"The map, right?" Benny asked.

"Right!" Henry answered. "It seems to me the map disappeared right after Sam cleaned the rooms yesterday. Maybe that's how our trash wound up in the Dumpster. Do you think Sam saw the map, figured out where the cabin was, then spent the morning looking for it after going to town?"

"I'm going to get to the bottom of this," Jessie said.

Jessie caught up to Sam outside. He was heading to the staff lodgings. "Hello, Sam. I wanted to ask you something."

Sam kept right on walking. "What is it now? Does Mrs. Crabtree need me? Why do you keep bothering me?"

Jessie bit her lip. She wasn't used to people being impatient with her. She looked Sam Jackson straight in the eye. "Did you clean our room yesterday and throw out a copy of a map when you were in there?"

Sam's eyes darkened. He started to move away. "I don't have any idea what you're talking about. I clean rooms. I don't throw out people's possessions. Or maybe you're suggesting I stole something from your room. Is that it?"

Jessie wasn't sure what to say. "No, I didn't mean that. I'm sorry I mentioned it.

I just wanted to find out if you knew anything about a map, that's all."

Sam was silent.

"Sam denied knowing anything about the map," Jessie said when she rejoined her sister and brothers inside. "I hope I didn't make him out to be a careless worker or a thief if he's not. Maybe I shouldn't have said anything at all."

"Well, maybe it wasn't Sam. Maybe it was Mr. Crabtree," Henry said.

"Since we're finished with work now," Violet began, "can we go for a walk? We haven't been to the Upper Basin area. There won't be too many tourists, since it's so misty and foggy out."

"Sure," Jessie said. "Then we can take another look at the map. Maybe we'll see where we made our wrong turn today."

The children walked by Old Faithful, then strolled to the Upper Basin area, where dozens of small geysers gurgled and steamed. The Aldens watched the hot springs from the wooden walkways. Clouds of steam gently rose from the ground. All the fog made it hard to see more than a few feet ahead.

"It's pretty out here, even in the fog," Violet said. "Can we walk a little farther? I like looking at the smaller geysers. Some of the colors of the hot springs are so pretty."

Jessie took Benny's hand. "Careful around here, Benny. Let's not walk too fast. It would be dangerous to slip off these walkways."

The Aldens seemed to be alone. Everything was blanketed in mist from the fog and from the hot springs bubbling nearby. The children stood by a railing, looking and listening to the odd little pools of water that simmered like teakettles on a stove.

"Shhh," Benny whispered suddenly. "Somebody else is on this walkway. I hear voices. But it's so foggy, I can't see who it is."

The Aldens stood still.

"Those kids saw the map," the children heard a man's voice say. "What if they get up there before we do?"

A woman's voice answered. "We have to

keep that from happening. I'll report to work early tomorrow and sign up for trail cleanup. Meet me at the trailhead at seven. We're so close. We can't let anyone get there first. . . . What's the matter?"

The two voices were silent for a few seconds.

The man finally answered. "I'm worried about my job. I haven't been around much. Everything is taking much longer than I thought."

"Don't worry," the young woman said. "I know the head manager at the lodge. I'll tell him I need you for trail work. Maybe they can put those kids on your job tomorrow morning instead. I'll get you back by afternoon."

The Aldens heard footsteps coming toward them. They tiptoed down the boardwalk, careful not to make noise. Once they got past the foggy hot springs area, the air cleared. They looked back at the mist still covering the walkways.

Out of the mist walked two people: Sam Jackson and Ranger Crowe.

CHAPTER 9

A Bear Scare

The children woke up at six the next morning.

"No slugabed Aldens today!" Jessie said a few minutes after she woke up. "We have to be at the front desk at six-thirty."

While the other children stirred and stretched, Jessie reread the note they had found taped to their door the night before.

Dear Aldens,
Change of plans. Can you work in the morning instead of the afternoon? If so, please meet

the manager, Mr. Colter, at the front desk, at
6:30. If you have other plans, don't worry. It's
your vacation! Happy treasure hunting. See you
Thursday. Lester and I are off tomorrow.

Eleanor Crabtree

"It looks like Ranger Crowe got in touch
with Mrs. Crabtree after all," Henry said.
"And that Sam is on the trails with her."

By six-thirty, the Aldens had finished a
breakfast of pancakes and sausages. They
gathered in the lobby to meet Mr. Colter.

"I like working here, but I wish we could
go hiking instead," Benny said. "What if
Sam Jackson finds the cabin before we do?
Or Mr. Crabtree does?"

Jessie bent down to talk with Benny.
"Know what? There are four of us Aldens
and only one Sam Jackson, one Ranger
Crowe, and one Mr. Crabtree. Remember
what Mrs. Crabtree said? We have four
pairs of eyes. We'll go hiking again first
thing this afternoon. I promise."

A minute later, a jolly man with a big
smile came over to the Aldens. "Let me

guess who you folks are," the man said in a booming voice. "The Aldens, right? I'm Bob Colter. I heard all about you from Eleanor. I hope you don't mind the change of plans. This morning our guides need some extra help giving a children's nature tour out at the West Thumb geyser areas. I heard a rumor that you are good at taking care of young people."

Benny looked up at the man. "That's because *we* are young people," he told Mr. Colter. "And we know lots about nature, even geysers. Especially Jessie. She knows everything."

This tickled Mr. Colter. "So I heard. Anyway, the tour is only a couple of hours long. You'll have the rest of the day free. Well, come along. The van is leaving for West Thumb at seven."

Benny stuck his thumb out. "West Thumb? Here's my west thumb, just like where we're going."

The Aldens spent the morning helping the guides lead a group of children around

the West Thumb Paint Pots near Yellowstone Lake. The young children on the tour
loved having the Aldens along. And Benny
was right. Jessie knew everything — almost,
anyway.

Riding back in the van, Henry had a good
idea. "We're passing the Continental Divide
area soon, aren't we?" he asked the van
driver.

The driver nodded. "We're about five
minutes away. Why?"

Henry leaned over so the driver could
hear him. "My brother and sisters and I
would like to get off there. We want to hike
on this end of the Lost Cabin Trails if
they're open. Then we'd only have a one-
way hike back to the lodge."

"Sure thing," the driver said. "I'll pull
into the parking lot."

In a few minutes, the van slowed down.
"Here's the spot," the driver told Henry.
"Looks as if the trails are open. I'll drop
you off. You folks have plenty of water,
food, and all your hiking gear?"

Henry held up his bulging backpack. "We

Aldens don't even go on a nature walk without all our outdoor supplies. Thanks a lot. Oh, would you tell Mr. Colter we decided to go hiking?"

"No problem," the driver said. "Happy hiking."

For a while the Aldens had very happy hiking indeed. Their backpacks were filled with plenty of water and trail mix. The hike began at the top of the mountain and went down. Best of all, they had the copy of Oz's map safe in Henry's pocket.

"This is an easy hike," Benny announced, now that he was an experienced hiker. "It's downhill. No huffing and puffing."

The Aldens had plenty of time to chat as they went along. Today they weren't the least bit out of breath.

"Do you think we'll run into Sam and Ranger Crowe?" Violet asked. "I'm worried that Sam saw our map. What if he made a copy for himself or figured out where the lost cabin might be?"

Everyone was quiet for a second until Jessie spoke up. "Sam might have Oz's trapper's map. I don't like to think so, but he seems so unfriendly whenever we talk about hiking. Last night when he worked with us, he only talked with the children, never to us."

"He talked to me," Benny said. "He said, 'Your turn' when we were playing Old Maid."

Everyone laughed. Sam Jackson wasn't much of a talker.

After about twenty minutes of hiking, the children reached a rocky ledge that overlooked a clear, still lake.

"The lake looks like a mirror for the sky," Violet said. "I wish I had my paints with me."

They looked up at the cliffs to see if any birds were nesting up there.

"A bald eagle!" Jessie whispered. She didn't want to frighten away the bird soaring in the air currents above her.

With the binoculars, the children took turns tracking the huge eagle.

Henry followed the flight of the graceful bird, hoping to see its mate. "Oh. I don't believe it," he said a few seconds later. "Look."

"What, Henry? What?" Jessie asked.

Henry slipped the binoculars from his neck. "Up there on that cliff. Isn't that Mr. Crabtree? Whoever it is has on that same bright orange hat. It must be him."

Jessie aimed the binoculars up the cliff. She focused the lenses. "It's got to be Mr. Crabtree! Wait! I think he just saw us."

The four children waved and jumped up and down to get Mr. Crabtree's attention. When they stopped, the orange-hatted hiker had moved from the cliff trail.

The children gathered up their packs. Henry tightened the straps for Benny and Violet. "He didn't wave back. Maybe that wasn't Mr. Crabtree after all," he said. "Remember, he told Mrs. Crabtree that he wouldn't hike very far from the parking lot? That cliff is pretty far away to be hiking alone. I guess we should get moving, too. We're not even halfway there yet."

Jessie studied the copy of Oz's map. "We're almost where the arrow shows the lost cabin might be. See, Henry? Here's the cliff. There's the turnoff for Handkerchief Lake. The problem is, I can't tell if the lost cabin is right off this trail or hidden in the deep woods."

Henry took his position at the head of the line. The children hiked single file through the narrow, wooded trail.

"Let's go a little farther, okay?" Henry suggested. "Benny, you and I can check the left side of the trail. Jessie and Violet can look to the right. Look for any unusual large shapes or forms. If no one's discovered the cabin, it might be buried under trees or vines after all these years."

The children saw fallen trees and unusual rocks, but no cabin. Soon the trail led into deep woods again.

"Grrr," came a sound nearby.

The Aldens froze in their spots.

"Grrr," came the sound again, this time much louder.

Henry clapped his hands. "Ring your bells, everybody!" he shouted.

Behind the other children, Jessie grabbed

a big branch with dry leaves. She banged it against a tree trunk. "Make lots of noise," she told everyone. "In case it is a . . . a . . . bear!"

"Back away slowly," Henry yelled. "The sound is coming from farther ahead on the trail below the cliff. Keep ringing your bear bells. Let's talk and shout while we're backing away. Maybe the bear will head in the other direction."

The growls seemed louder. Was the bear coming closer or just getting madder? The children heard the crunch of something moving in the woods. Whatever it was, it sounded huge.

With their bear bells ringing, the children yelled and shouted.

"No running!" Jessie advised. "Just smooth walking. Don't be nervous. It's probably more scared of us than we are of it."

When Benny heard another round of growls, he yelled out, "My legs are all rubbery."

That's when Jessie began to sing at the

top of her lungs. "The bear went over the mountain, the bear went over the mountain. The bear went over the mountain, to see what he could see."

Pretty soon the other children joined in. They shook their bear bells. They sang the bear song over and over until they reached the end of the trail, back where they had started.

"Whew," Henry said, when they reached the lookout area. "That was a close call."

"Let's sit down on this picnic bench," Jessie suggested. "I need to rest my legs."

Benny took off his pack. "Look, my knees are knocking together from seeing that bear."

The other children stared at Benny.

"You *saw* the bear?" Violet asked. Her throat was completely dry, and her words nearly faded away.

Benny looked up at his brother and sisters. "Well . . . I almost saw the bear."

"Hey, Aldens," they heard a familiar voice call out from a tour bus parked nearby. "Need a ride?"

Henry stood up. "Grandfather! What are you doing here?"

"I'm on my way back from my fishing trip," he told his grandchildren. "Some folks wanted to stop to take pictures by the Continental Divide sign. I guess I should ask what you are doing here, though I can see by your backpacks that you've been hiking."

"Hiking and going the opposite direction from a bear," Jessie told her grandfather.

"We saw a bear. I mean, I *almost* saw a bear," Benny said. "But I wasn't scared. Know why? Because I had on these." Benny held out his arm and jingled his bear bells.

Mr. Alden laughed. "That's the best bear repellent I know. Now, unless you want to hike all the way back to the lodge, hop on this tour bus. I want my companions to hear all about your bear stories. Then we can tell you all about our fish stories."

The Aldens boarded the bus. They were so busy entertaining Mr. Alden's new travel companions that they didn't notice a famil- iar car pulling out of the crowded parking

lot right after the bus. All the way up and down the mountain roads, an old red car stayed right behind the tour bus.

When the bus arrived at the lodge, Mr. Colter was standing out front to greet the passengers. "So you're the grandfather of these splendid children," he said to Mr. Alden. "We've had nothing but praise for them from everyone on our staff and all the guests who've met them."

Mr. Colter turned to Benny. "I see you're back from your hike safe and sound."

"Almost not safe and sound!" Benny cried. "We saw a bear. I mean, we almost saw a bear. But we *heard* a bear for sure."

"Whew, Benny," Mr. Colter said after Benny repeated his story. "That sounds like a close call. Oh, Mrs. Crabtree," he added when he noticed Mrs. Crabtree had joined the group. "You and your husband are back early. How did you two enjoy your day in Cody?"

Mrs. Crabtree was still smiling from hearing about Benny's adventure. "Oh, I went to Cody alone. It was wonderful. Lester stayed behind to work on our trailer. He's been there all day."

"All day?" Jessie said, before she had time to think. "Oops." She covered her mouth.

Mrs. Crabtree looked puzzled. "What is it, Jessie? Did you see Lester today?"

The Aldens weren't sure what to say.

"Oh, we thought we saw Mr. Crabtree when we were hiking up by the Continental Divide."

Mrs. Crabtree smoothed her jacket nervously. "Oh, no. Mr. Crabtree spent the whole day at our trailer. Not that he got much done, mind you. It was his day off, after all. But he just told me he stayed in all day."

"Oh," Jessie said. She suddenly made herself very busy adjusting the straps on her backpack.

Just then Oz Elkhorn appeared. "There you are, Jimmy. And your grandkids, too. Mr. Colter said you'd be pulling up any second. I had a few errands up this way. I thought I'd wait around to tell you some good news."

"What's that?" the Aldens all said at once.

Grinning from ear to ear, Oz reached into his canvas bag. He pulled out a tube of paper and unrolled it.

"You found the trapper's map!" Jessie cried.

"Nope, it found me," Oz said, shaking his head. "I'm not sure how. I don't suppose any of you children stuck this map in my mailbox here at the inn?"

"No way," Henry said. "We haven't seen that map since the day we arrived at Yellowstone. All we have is this beat-up copy that landed in the Dumpster." Henry pulled out the Aldens' copy of the map to show Oz.

"Good!" Oz told the children. "Now we have two maps. We're going to need them for our hike tomorrow."

"What hike?" Violet asked.

"Our hike to the lost cabin," Oz said. "It's about time we found that place. I'm taking the day off from the store. I'll meet you bright and early."

CHAPTER 10

A Secret in the Snow

At six A.M. the next morning, it was early, but it wasn't bright the way Oz had expected. Jessie woke up first, as she often did. The room looked strange — dim and more quiet than usual.

She tiptoed to the window. "Snow!" she whispered, forgetting that everyone was asleep.

The word *snow* was magic to Benny. Suddenly he was as wide awake as if it were the middle of the day.

"Snow?" he said.

By this time, the other children were awake, too. They joined Jessie by the window. Sure enough, flakes of snow were falling over everything.

"It can't be snowing," Violet said. "It's July."

"But it *is* snowing," Jessie said, smiling at the thought of summer snow. "The guidebook says it can snow almost any time of the year in Yellowstone."

"That means snowflakes for breakfast," Benny said. "We just have to stick our tongues out. Can we go outside before it melts? I never saw snow in the summer."

"I'm already getting my socks on," Jessie said.

In no time flat, all four Aldens were outside the Old Faithful Inn. They stuck their tongues out to catch the snowflakes. And the children drew their initials in the few inches of snow on the ground.

"Now I need hot chocolate," Benny declared after a while. "And hot waffles, too. Let's go inside for breakfast."

"Hey, Aldens," the children heard when

they entered the lobby. "I hope you folks will be ready for our hike in half an hour."

The children turned around. Across the lobby stood Mr. Alden and Oz Elkhorn, bundled head to toe in parkas, hats, and mittens. Next to them were several sets of snowshoes.

"Are those for our hike?" Benny asked.

"They sure are," Oz said. "This is going to be a real treat. A snow hike in July. I arranged it with the weatherman, just for the Alden family," he said, winking at Mr. Alden. "I'm told there's already a foot of snow on the upper trails."

Snowplows made their way up and down the mountains just as if it were the middle of winter.

"See," Oz told the children from the driver's seat of his truck, "in Yellowstone we're always ready for any kind of weather. We keep our snow tires on all year long."

Awhile later, Oz pulled into the Continental Divide lookout area. "Hmmm. Some hikers are already here," he said when he noticed a snow-covered car and truck parked at the end of the lot. "Judging by all the snow on them, it looks as if they've been here awhile."

Indeed, Oz and the Aldens spotted snow-shoe prints in the trails as well. Soon they, too, were deep in the woods.

"Snow hiking goes fast. No bumps," Benny said. "It's easier to see everything better. Like bears and stuff," he added.

"Somebody must have been pretty determined to get out here this early," Oz said later. "I thought we'd have caught up with these hikers by now. Whoever's out here must be moving like antelopes through these trails. These tracks seem to be heading in the same direction as we want to go."

The six hikers set off on the trail again. After a while, the snow tapered off. In the distance, everyone could see the sun begin to peek out between the clouds.

When the sky finally cleared, Oz pointed down to the valley. "Here, Benny. Take a look in my binoculars. They're focused already. Just point them down that way."

Benny did as he was told. "Hey! I can see all the way down to the Old Faithful Inn!"

Leading the hikers, Oz called out the names of the different types of trees. He saw small animals way before the children did, and he named every one.

"Did you see that muskrat?" he asked Jessie and Benny when a creature scurried by.

"It just went behind that big lump of snow over there," Benny said. "Hey! Isn't a big lump what we're looking for?"

Off in the distance, everyone could see what Benny was talking about. Some pine trees had toppled over something — a rock or more fallen trees. It was hard to tell.

"Good eyes, Benny," Jessie said. "And look at the tracks leading over there, too."

Oz put his fingers to his lips. Everyone stood as still as snow sculptures. At first all they heard was the wind. But the longer they stood, the more they could make out voices in the distance.

"It sounds like a bunch of people talking in there," Benny whispered.

"Let's check it out," Oz said.

Everyone swooshed over the snow. The voices grew louder. A few feet from the mound of fallen trees, Oz and the Aldens not only heard loud voices, they heard words.

"Please show us that bag," a woman's voice pleaded.

Another voice interrupted. "My sister and I think that bag might have belonged to our great-great-great-grandfather. You can check if you don't believe me. *The Tale of the Lost Cabin Miners* tells all about him. His name was Samuel Jackson Crowe."

The woman spoke up next. "Sam's right. We have some old family journals that mention this cabin and a leather pouch the miners left behind. One of those miners was our ancestor."

There was no doubt about the next voice. "Nonsense!" Mr. Crabtree said. "Anybody could read that book and say they were related to gold miners. In fact, everybody in Yellowstone has probably read that book. What's to keep me from saying my ancestors were those miners? Anyway, I'm the one who found the leather pouch, not the two of you."

"It's time to go in there," Oz told the Aldens. "Nobody'd even be here if it weren't for my granddad's map!"

Oz and the Aldens began to pull away a pile of pine branches covering the hump.

"The cabin!" Benny yelled when he uncovered a doorway.

"Who's there?" Mr. Crabtree called out. "Is there a tour bus coming through here all of a sudden?"

Even Oz had to laugh. "Of course not, Lester. It's me and the Aldens — hardly a tour bus."

The hut was so small that Oz and the Aldens had to stand outside to talk to everyone inside: Ranger Crowe, Sam Jackson, and Lester Crabtree.

Oz smiled at the two young people. "I hope Lester's not giving you a hard time. I won't, either. But can you tell us all what's going on?"

Before anyone else answered, Lester

Crabtree interrupted. "What's going on? I'll tell you what's going on. I got here practically in the middle of the night. Then, not long after, these two arrive, and now you six people. It's too close for comfort in here."

Mr. Alden spoke up now. "Well, what's everyone arguing about? After all, the lost cabin isn't lost anymore."

Everyone stepped out of the cabin to settle matters.

Lester Crabtree was holding on to a leather pouch, about the size of a schoolbag. Suddenly Sam made a grab for it, and five or six yellowish rocks rolled onto the snow.

Mr. Crabtree bent down. "These aren't gold!" he said in a disgusted voice. "They're just a bunch of plain old Yellowstone rocks."

Oz Elkhorn couldn't help smiling. "That's why Yellowstone is called 'Yellowstone,' Lester. I hope none of you folks was counting on getting rich from what was in this bag. Looks as if those lost miners didn't leave much behind but this old hut."

Sam Jackson picked up the leather pouch. He looked inside. "Hey, there are some old papers in here, too. Look, Emily," he said to Ranger Crowe.

Everyone crowded around to see what Sam Jackson had found.

Sam began reading:

"The unforgiving Yellowstone winter is over at last. The deep snows are melting. We begin the next leg of our trip back to Missouri today, six months after our terrible journey through these mysterious mountains. We leave behind our dreams and return to our old farmland. Samuel Jackson Crowe, 1850."

"Samuel Jackson Crowe?" Jessie asked Sam. "Is that *your* full name?"

Sam clutched the old, yellowed paper in his hand. "That is my name. This is my sister, Emily Jackson Crowe. I just used my middle name Jackson out here. Emily and I were afraid that if everyone realized we were a brother and sister with the last name Crowe, they would figure out that we were

searching for the lost cabin. So we didn't tell anyone we were related."

Ranger Crowe looked upset when she saw all the puzzled faces. "I started working in Yellowstone last year. I knew my ancestor had been a gold miner, but not a successful one. He wound up a poor farmer in Missouri. But then I started hearing stories about some miners leaving gold behind in this old cabin. So I got Sam to come out here, too, so we could look for the cabin together. Now it looks as if our relative just left this bag of rocks."

Oz took off his hat and unzipped his jacket. "It looks as if your relative played a funny joke on you folks. Now I have to ask you two, did you steal my map? That didn't belong to you or your relatives. It belonged to *my* relative — Granddad, then my cousin, then me. Nobody else had any business with that map."

Sam looked down at his snowshoes. "I took the map when I realized you'd left it in the copier. I know I shouldn't have. As soon as I discovered you had a mailbox at the inn, I returned it there when no one was looking."

Ranger Crowe didn't look any happier than her brother. "Sam was the one I let through the gates when you arrived in Yellowstone," she explained. "I was allowed to let him go through, of course, since he works in the park."

Jessie needed to know something. "Did you put the sign up saying the trail was closed?"

Ranger Crowe explained. "This summer, I signed up for all the trail-clearing duty. I worked so hard at it, I was put in charge. Whenever I was out working on the trails, I put up the sign. I didn't want someone else to find the cabin when we were so close. And I changed the markers, too. There are plenty of other hiking trails around here, anyway."

Benny listened to all this, but he needed to know more. "What about our map? Oz made a copy, just for us. Henry found it in the Dumpster."

Sam looked Benny straight in the eye. "I

guess it could have fallen off of the dresser and into the trash. But I didn't notice it when I emptied the trash can into the Dumpster. I just did my job."

"Same here," Mr. Crabtree said, "though I wouldn't have minded using a map instead of my brains to find this cabin. I've been looking for this place every summer since I started coming out here with Eleanor."

The children looked at each other, full of questions.

"But why did you tell Mrs. Crabtree you weren't hiking yesterday? She said you told her you were in your trailer all day. But we saw you through our binoculars, right before our bear scare."

Mr. Crabtree looked more upset than Sam and Emily Crowe put together. "Well, I might as well tell the rest of the story," he went on. "Eleanor doesn't care much for hiking, so I go by myself. I know I shouldn't go too far in the woods alone. But once I had a bee in my bonnet about the lost cabin, I kept going farther and farther on the trails. I just didn't want to tell

Eleanor about hiking alone, you understand?"

Everyone was smiling now, except Mr. Crabtree.

"There, there, Lester," Oz said. "If you don't want Eleanor to know about this, we don't have to mention it. After all, you found the cabin, and you're safe and sound. No harm done."

Mr. Crabtree pulled down the brim of his orange hat. Without looking up, he continued talking. "Well, there is some harm done to these four children," he said, turning to the Aldens. "And it has to do with bears."

"You saw a bear!" Benny cried.

Mr. Crabtree loosened the straps of his backpack and dropped it to the ground. He reached inside. Everyone heard a button click on. "*Grrr,*" they heard next. "*Grrr.*" The growls were followed by some thuds and the sounds of snapping branches.

Everyone but Mr. Crabtree felt prickles of fear on the backs of their necks.

"This tape recorder is the bear you heard," Mr. Crabtree said. He held up a portable tape recorder and showed it to everyone. Mr. Crabtree pressed another button. "There. I'm erasing this. I made this bear tape to keep hikers away from here, especially after I saw the four of you come down from the trails the other afternoon when I was up on the porch of the inn. I knew I was getting closer to the cabin, and I just wanted to find it once and for all. I owe everyone an apology."

"But there was a bear," Benny insisted. "I know there was."

Everyone looked at each other and smiled. There was no way of checking on Benny's bear.

Benny jiggled his bear bells. "See these? They scared away our bear, and it never came back."

"*Grrr,*" Jessie said, putting her arms around Benny. "Have a bear hug."

GERTRUDE CHANDLER WARNER discovered when she was teaching that many readers who like an exciting story could find no books that were both easy and fun to read. She decided to meet this need, and her first book, *The Boxcar Children*, quickly proved she had succeeded.

Miss Warner drew on her own experiences to write the mystery. As a child she spent hours watching trains go by on the tracks opposite her family home. She often dreamed about what it would be like to set up housekeeping in a caboose or freight car — the situation the Alden children find themselves in.

When Miss Warner received requests for more adventures involving Henry, Jessie, Violet, and Benny Alden, she began additional stories. In each, she chose a special setting and introduced unusual or eccentric characters who liked the unpredictable.

While the mystery element is central to each of Miss Warner's books, she never thought of them as strictly juvenile mysteries. She liked to stress the Aldens' independence and resoucefulness and their solid New England devotion to using up and making do. The Aldens go about most of their adventures with as little adult supervision as possible — something else that delights young readers.

Miss Warner lived in Putnam, Connecticut, until her death in 1979. During her lifetime, she received hundreds of letters from girls and boys telling her how much they liked her books.